dancing
for
danger

a meggy tale

dancing for danger

a meggy tale

Stoddart Kids

TORONTO • NEW YORK

There's a rare beauty
in something hidden and secret
and it's a rare education
to be gotten
in hidden places.

FROM *AWAY*, BY JANE URQUHART

Published in Canada in 2000 by
Stoddart Kids,
a division of Stoddart Publishing Co. Limited
34 Lesmill Road
Toronto, ON M3B 2T6
Tel (416) 445-3333 Fax (416) 445-5967
E-mail cservice@genpub.com

Published in the United States in 2001 by
Stoddart Kids,
a division of Stoddart Publishing Co. Limited
180 Varick Street, 9th Floor
New York, New York 10014
Toll free 1-800-805-1083
E-mail gdsinc@genpub.com

Distributed in Canada by
General Distribution Services
325 Humber College Blvd.,
Toronto, ON M9W 7C3
Tel (416) 213-1919 Fax (416) 213-1917
E-mail cservice@genpub.com

Distributed in the United States by
General Distribution Services
4500 Witmer Industrial Estates, PMB 128
Niagara Falls, New York 14305-1386
Toll free 1-800-805-1083
E-mail gdsinc@genpub.com

03 02 01 00   01 02 03 04

CANADIAN CATALOGUING IN PUBLICATION DATA

Griffin, Margot
Dancing for danger

A Meggy tale.
ISBN 0-7737-6136-5

I. Burden, P. John, 1943–   . II. Title.

PS8563.R5352D36 2000   jC813.6   C00-931097-5
PZ7.G74Da 2000

A chapter book about one of Ireland's forbidden hedge schools,
and the children who attended it, over two hundred years ago.

Cover Design: P. John Burden
Text Design: Tannice Goddard

*We acknowledge for their financial support of our publishing program the
Government of Canada through the Book Publishing Industry Development
Program (BPIDP), the Canada Council, and the Ontario Arts Council.*

Printed and bound in Canada

A person would be fortunate to have one dear 'Da'.
My life has been blessed with three.
First and for-ever, my own beloved dad, Russ Walker,
whom I can still hear singing me Toora Loora.
Second, J. B. Griffin, my father-in-law,
the sweetest gentleman this side of Dublin.
May they both be up in heaven now,
sharing a drop of the 'creature'.
The third 'Da' is my husband Phil,
who is the kind of devoted, loving father most
women could only hope their daughters would have.
— M.G.

To Margot, Kathryn, and Robin.
Thank you for your patience.
— P.J.B.

contents

FOREWORD

Have you ever felt afraid to go to school because you thought a bully might hurt you, maybe even with a gun or a knife? Did you ever worry that your school would close and you might never see your classmates or favorite teacher again?

Away back in time — more than two hundred years ago and far across the Atlantic Ocean — there were children in Ireland who felt those very same fears. The government of the time made up a set of unfair laws called the Penal Code. Those laws gave property and power to Protestants and the English, while denying power and civil rights to the children's families, just because they were Irish Catholics (even though they made up 75% of the population). Many Catholics refused to obey laws that forbade them to educate their children in their own language and religion.

Schoolmasters were forbidden to teach, so they searched for secret places to hold their schools. A family's home could be burned if they allowed the master to teach classes there. Children and others were offered money to betray their own parents, relatives, and neighbors who were involved in keeping the secret schools going. Still, many worked secretly together to keep the master fed, sheltered, and safe.

Often, a schoolhouse was built — a sod house scooped out of the bank of the roadside by the community. Inside this dark, damp, hedge school, students would sit on rocks to learn their lessons, with only a bit of fire to warm them and cast poor light on their slates.

Every illegal lesson, every forbidden story, was precious because it could be disrupted at any time by law officers or informers. Each day a student was chosen for the role of lookout. The child stood hidden, some way off from the school, prepared to give a warning if enemies approached.

Choosing to be a teacher meant living a dangerous life. Masters caught teaching could be fined, beaten, jailed, deported, or worse. When the soldiers came, they ran to a secret mountain hiding place. Sometimes the pupils had narrow escapes when they were helping the master get away.

The brave teachers, children, and families who risked so much to keep their Irish education alive, would have understood your fears. In hidden schools across Ireland they were the kind of heroes who lived every day, finding a way to keep their beliefs alive.

I wondered what it would have been like to be a young girl living in beautiful Ireland during that fearful time. My main character, Meggy, came to answer my questions. Leaning close to my ear, she whispered her story to me in her lilting voice. Even during those dark and difficult times Meggy found ways to love, laugh, and learn.

1

the hiding school

Meggy was always the first child there. She stood stock still, ignoring the damp Irish mist as her green eyes searched out every hedge and hollow to be sure no soldiers or informers were lurking about. Then, she did what would have appeared daft to those not in the know. She knocked softly on the bank of clay by the roadside. As it opened inward, the spot where she had knocked was revealed to be a well-disguised door.

She ducked her head and scooted through the door, closing it quickly behind her. "Welcome, Meggy, to the finest hedge school in all of County Kerry," said a voice filled half with truth and half with humor.

As her eyes adjusted to the cave-like dark, Meggy

bobbed her head politely and responded, "Mornin', Master Cleary, and sure aren't I glad to be here today?"

Then, and only then, a small freckled face popped out mischievously from behind Meggy's skirts saucily echoing her, "Mornin', Master Cleary, and aren't I *not* sure that I'm glad to be here today?" and disappeared again.

Master Cleary winked at Meggy and questioned her seriously. "Meggy, could it be that you've grown a head from out of your waist since our last class?"

This brought the face and the rest of Meggy's little brother out from behind her. He indignantly announced, "Why it's me, Master! It's me, Danny. Meggy couldn't grow another head."

The three of them laughed, small chuckle clouds filling the cold morning air between them. The master knew that wherever Meggy went, Danny went. And Meggy knew few girls her age were lucky enough to still be at school. She was aware that she was being allowed to stay on only to keep watch over young Dan during these dangerous times. If poor, wee Michael hadn't died, one week to the day after he was born, she would be home with her mam, helping with the babe and the chores.

The master rubbed his hands together and said, "I've been tryin' to decide whether to light the fire or not.

Sure, and it's chilly enough for a spring morn. But with the informers sneakin' about, we don't want the smoke to be givin' away the location of our fine learnin' establishment."

As he threw his arms out regally to indicate the mud hut their families had dug out of the roadbank, Meggy wished that her fine schoolmaster had the fine school he deserved. Even though the cuffs of his black coat were frayed and the knees of his breeches roughly mended, Master Cleary's shirt was snowy white and he wore his black hat with dignity.

He stood there, silent for a moment, with his eyes closed. Meggy couldn't help but wonder if he was picturing himself on a fine, wooden desk chair, instead of the barrel that was his perch of higher learning. And wouldn't it be fine if the rocks and hobs she and the other children sat their skinny bottoms on would magically turn into rows of tidy desks?

But a loud knock at the door startled Meggy and the master from their bit of daydreaming. Even Danny tensed with fear until the door was shoved open by a familiar tumble of impatient students. Meggy quickly claimed the low rock by the door for her and Dan. There were only two dozen or so stones and hobs. Others would sit on the ash-covered floor. The tall and the tardy would stand at the back.

Meggy pitied the ones who straggled in late. They had already walked miles just to get to school and now there was no room to even sit down. She pulled Danny, protesting onto her knee, and slid over to make room for her friend Fiona, whose raggedy skirt drooped with the damp.

The others filed in, most leaving two pieces of turf by the door as part of their payment for the day's learning. Some presented the master with a few eggs or potatoes. Meggy knew that meant there'd be less to fill the families' own hungry bellies that day.

Master Cleary said, "Well, that settles it. We can't waste good turf. We'll have a bit of fire to take the mornin's chill out of our bones." As the first wisps of smoke escaped the hole in the center of the roof, Meggy worried whose eyes might set upon it.

Before everyone resettled closer to the fire's warmth, and the master even had a chance to ask, Roddy McSorley burst out, "Sir! Sir! Bein' the biggest and the strongest here, I think I should be the lookout for today!"

Meggy squeezed Danny so hard that he wriggled down off her lap to sit on the floor and leaned back against her legs. She was half cross with the pushy Roddy and half cross with herself for being so lady-like in waiting to be asked, that she missed the opportunity to be the lookout again. She nudged Fiona

and whispered, "What does big and strong have to do
with bein' lookout anyway? He just wants to be gettin'
out of the lessons."

"The big, lazy amadon. He'll probably fall asleep on
the job," replied the usually sweet-spoken Fiona.

But the master patted Roddy on the shoulder and
said, "That's a stand-up Irish lad. Now, what will be our
warnin' signal for today?"

"Tis the season of the cuckoo, Master, and I can do
a fine imitation of his call — koo-kooo, koo-kooo,"
bragged Roddy. As soon as he started kooing, Meggy

6

rolled her eyes at Fiona and they huddled together trying to hide their fits of giggles.

As Roddy strode out to take up his lookout post, he held his head so high and proud that he forgot to duck under the low door, and whacked his brow. Meggy couldn't restrain a snort of laughter at his expense. Before the others got too carried away, Master Cleary began reminding them of their jobs in case of discovery. "First, and most important, get yourselves and the little ones to safety. Second, if you have a chance, scoop up any books or slates you can carry. We don't want to be leavin' any evidence of learnin' behind, and besides, we'll need them again."

They had all heard these cautious instructions every morning for so long that most of them listened with only half an ear. But Meggy had overheard the men who met around their cottage table. They told the terrible tale of what happened to the last hedge school master who was discovered committing the crime of trying to educate children like herself.

The master's deep, rich voice interrupted her worries. "Now, let us get down to the business of learnin'. Good morning, lads and lassies. And why are you here today?"

Meggy led the others in responding, "Good mornin' to ye, Master Cleary. We are here today to exercise our brains."

"And exercise your brains you shall," said the master. "We have twice as much to cover today, for Master O'Flaherty, old Fancy Feet himself, will reach our village tonight and be here at our school on the morrow."

Meggy couldn't resist a burst of happy applause. "Who is Master O'Flaherty?" asked Dan.

Meggy's eyes sparked with anticipation as she answered. "He's the traveling dance master, a wee man who looks much like an overgrown leprechaun. And sure, doesn't he have the magic of the music in him?"

"That's enough of an explanation for now, Meggy. We all know you love the dancin', but that's tomorrow. Now it's time to be jiggin' with some numbers," said Master Cleary, as he led them into a whirlwind of lessons — arithmetic, geography, and spelling.

Meggy liked all the master's lessons. But she was always glad when spelling was over because then, each day just before the dinner break, Master Cleary would read aloud to them, one delicious chapter from one of the precious books he carried in his satchel.

Yesterday, Master had stopped right when that dashing rogue, Robin Hood, was surrounded by the evil Sheriff of Nottingham's men. Now, as Danny and the little ones were chanting their last dictation words together, "Rat, r-a-t spells rat," the master was already opening the green book.

It was as if the simple motion of lifting the cover cast a spell over all the students. Even the littlest ones didn't wiggle. Even twitchy Danny didn't twitch. Every child leaned closer and sat more still to hear each word that the master read. *"Would Robin of Locksley's last vision be the smug sneer on the Sheriff's face and the flash of silver before the lance pierced . . ."*

2

escape to the west

Roddy burst through the door without so much as the twitter of a cuckoo call, "Master, Master — I'm sorry — I don't know how they got so close — the landlord's troop — it is just over the hill!"

The quiet in the room changed from magic to fear. It was broken by the book falling from the master's hands, forgotten to the floor. "From which way are they comin', Roddy?"

"From the west, Sir."

"Stay calm, children. Remember your escape plan. You can trick them by circlin' round the stand of yews out front and then hidin' in your chosen spots to the west, from where they have come. Be off with

you! Godspeed."

Meggy could feel the others pushing impatiently behind her. They had played Escape to the East and to the West many times before, but today there were no giggles, only a few muffled cries. She gave Fiona's hand a strong squeeze and, holding Danny in front of her, moved quickly toward the door. She tripped on something. It was the master's book, *Robin Hood*. Without thinking, she shoved it in her apron pocket.

After a cautious look in all directions, Meggy grabbed Danny's hand and whispered, "Run like the wind to the yew trees." They had run to play in their shade many times before, but the distance never seemed so far as today.

Meggy tugged Dan to the center of the grove. She sandwiched him between herself and the bark of a giant tree. It took a minute for her to hear because her heart felt like it was pounding out of her ears. But then the *tramp, tramp* of the roughnecks' boots and the harsh sounds of their voices could be heard.

Meggy could also feel the trembling and shaking of the others hidden there. She was terrified the band of louts would hear their rapid breathing, or see some of the bigger lads who had climbed up into the branches.

The yew that sheltered Dan and herself was huge at its base. She remembered Da telling her it was likely a thousand years old. She wondered how many other frightened children this fortress-like stand had hidden.

Suddenly, she noticed the school door was slightly open — a dead giveaway. The last one out should have closed it. Where was Master Cleary?

"Now what do we have here?" asked a burly brute as he kicked the door in. Another five big bullies strode over to join him.

"An open door! How welcoming," mocked one. "Let's go in and show them that teach and learn here, what we think of their precious hedge school."

Like mad dogs to a bone, the hateful men shoved into the school, kicking and bashing and crashing. The minute they were all inside, the children raced from the temporary safety of the trees to their chosen shelters.

As Roddy ran past, Meggy heard him mutter, "I'd like to teach them a lesson or two."

Sneaking in spurts from tree to bush to boulder, Meggy led Danny to their hidey-hole. "Run, Dan, run! This may be the most important hide-and-seek game of our lives!"

Danny tumbled. Meggy scooped him up and carried him to the tunnel-like entrance in the thick hawthorn hedge. The last blooms were falling, but the thorns were sharp. She turned her back to the hedge and made sure no one saw them. Pulling her brother's back to her chest she warned, "Dan, close your eyes, cover your face with your hands, and curl up like a ball so the thorns won't pick you." For once, he did as she told him without yammering.

Meggy curled herself around him and backed into the prickly cave. When the thorny tunnel took a slight jog to the left she followed it a bit, and then sat down hidden in the heart of the hawthorn. They waited, trembling and catching their breath. Just when Meggy's sides stopped aching, a rush of footsteps padded close by. The sound was too soft for a soldier's boots. Meggy

said a silent prayer that the owner of the footsteps would soon find a place to hide.

She felt something warm and wet on her hands. Blood was trickling down Danny's bare little legs. The thorns had scratched him, but it was a smaller pain than what they might have received if the soldiers had caught them learning. Seeing the blood, Dan started to cry. "Hush, Dan. When we get home, I'll boil up the root of the Fairy Fingers plant and rub it on your poor, wee legs, so the fairies will take the hurt away."

Meggy ignored the long scratches on her own arms,

but she knew it would take more than fairies to take away the pain of seeing her school destroyed. They sat achingly still inside their nest of thorns, flinching with every soldier's curse and every crackle of twigs they heard. They sat there long after the rooster crowed the hour of their midday dinner break.

Finally it was so quiet you could hear the bees' song. Danny's stomach rumbled loudly in the silence. "I'm hungry . . . I want Mam . . . I want to go home."

Meggy rubbed his little belly and shifted him off her lap as she stood. "Stay put, Dan. I'll just take a look to see if all is clear." She inched her way back through the tunnel of thorns. Although she was brave in front of Dan, Meggy had to take three big breaths before she dared to peek her face out of their hidey-hole.

There was no sight or sound of the enemy. "Come quick, Dan. Stay close to the hedge. Follow it home — home to Mam."

3

home, safe home

When their humble thatched cottage finally came into view, it looked as wonderful as a castle to Meggy. She could see her mam worrying and watching for them behind the half door. Meggy's brave face started to crumple at the sight of her. By the time her mother had slammed and bolted both halves of the door and turned to pull them to her, Meggy and Danny were crying.

"Mam, Mam . . . the landlord's bullies came . . . they destroyed our school." Meggy's words came out muffled and breathless from the shelter of her mother's arms.

"Mam, Mam, Mam, Mam," was all that wee Dan could say, as he sobbed against her skirts.

"Oh, me darlin's, isn't it a terrible fright you've had?" comforted Mam, as she patted and hugged them over to the table. "You are safe at home now. Look what I've baked for you — some fine oaten bread, still warm from the griddle, and a nice cup of milk."

Meggy thought, "I'll never be able to swallow even a drop of milk." But the smell of warm bread, and the snug of their cottage, soon wrapped the safe feeling of home about her. All Mam had to do was feed Dan the first bit of fresh, buttered bread, and he was soon fully occupied stuffing his little tear-stained face.

18

As soon as she felt safe herself, Meggy's mind began to race with questions: What about the others — the master — Fiona?

Mam must have read her mind because she squeezed her hand and said, "Try not to worry yourself, Meggy. You got you and Dan home safely. We'll hear about the others soon enough. When news of your school's discovery reached us, your da went out to see what he and the other men could do." Mam believed a busy mind is a healthy mind, so she set Meggy to spinning and Dan to churning the butter. Meggy, sick with fear for her master and friends, spun as many frightening possibilities in her head as her fingers spun threads.

The afternoon seemed to grow longer and the cottage seemed to grow smaller as Danny pounded crankily on the churn and Meggy spun faster and faster at the wheel. Just when it seemed the walls would burst with the sound of the pounding and the size of Meggy's worries, Mam said, "Here comes your da now." She got up from her place by the hearth to let him in.

Da was a big man of little words. He sat down at the table and looking straight at Meggy said, "All your schoolmates are safe in their homes." Then he folded his big, rough hands and said the blessing.

Meggy knew her da didn't like any talking while he was taking his meal, but she couldn't hold back her question. "But Da, what about Master Cleary?"

Da looked up from his stew and said kindly, but firmly, "Later, Meggy. I'm sure we'll be hearin' about the master later." The worried family ate the rest of their meal in silence. As soon as it was done and cleaned up, Meggy set the root of the Fairy Fingers to boil and then helped Mam pull out the settle bed. She helped Dan off with his shoes and socks and hung his breeches on the hook for the morrow, while he crawled into bed. Despite the day he'd had, Dan was sound asleep before Meggy had even finished gently soothing the broth of the Fairy Fingers onto his thorn-scratched legs.

Only as she began to undress herself, did she rediscover the book she'd carried in her apron pocket all afternoon. As Meggy ran her fingers over the fine, green cover with its gold lettering, she uttered a fervent wish, "Oh, wouldn't it be grand to own a book such as this!" But she had heard her da tell the other men, when they were hiring Master Cleary, how lucky they were to get a schoolmaster with such a fine collection of books. She could remember her father's exact words. "It would take all me earnin's from a whole week's work just to buy the geography book."

Meggy opened the cover and saw Master Cleary's name written in his own fine script. She slammed the book shut. She knew her whole family would be endan-

gered if the soldiers searched their house and found
this evidence of the schoolmaster. Meggy's mind raced.
Where could she hide it? She heard the chickens
rustling. Clever Mam had sewn up a wee curtain for
them that hung down from the bench built against the
side wall. A quick look showed that her parents were at
the table talking with their heads close together.

Quickly, Meggy crouched down in front of the hens'
cubbies. Talking softly to them, "Night, night birdies,
sleep tight birdies," she tucked the precious book in
between the straw of their nests.

Meggy tiptoed back across the cold clay floor in her bare feet, and had just slipped in beside Dan, when a knock came at the door. She pulled the quilt up to her chin and prayed, "Please, don't let it be the enemy lookin' for the master." Da opened the top half of the door, just a crack, to reveal Roddy McSorley and his father. They talked in guarded whispers at the door.

Then they were gone, and Da turned back looking so serious, Meggy was almost afraid to hear his words. "The bad news is what we knew already. The school has been discovered and it is a scene of dismal destruction. You will never have lessons there again." Meggy held her breath, listening, and wishing that her da was a man of even fewer words. "The good news, Meggy, is that your master is clever beyond book learnin'. Sure, and didn't he outsmart those unscrupulous scoundrels? He stood up on his barrel and hauled himself up through the smoke hole. Then he lay flat on the roof, coverin' himself with branches he'd left up there for that very purpose. Now off to sleep with ye, lass. You're a brave girl and a fine sister to Dan."

As Da leaned over to give her a rare kiss on the forehead, she looked up at him and asked, "Da, will we ever have school again?"

"Yes, Meggy love, your master is not givin' in to those

bullies yet. He passed on the message that those who can are to meet him, two mornin's from now under the Crankanny tree, where the stony books are stacked."

4

❖

WHERE THE STONY BOOKS
ARE STACKED

When Danny woke and heard the news, he thought it was a fine idea to have a holiday and then have school outside. Mam said, "I'm not at all sure it is safe for the two of you to be goin' off that far away and then havin' classes out in the open."

Da spoke. "The master has chosen the spot for learnin' wisely. It is well off the road, protected on one side by the lake, and a cliff on the other. Besides, ye don't want our children to grow up brainless, do ye now?"

Meggy, who couldn't wait to get back to her friend Fiona, her lessons, and especially Master Cleary and his stories, reassured her mother, "Don't be frettin' yourself,

Mam. Didn't I get Dan and meself safe home last time? I can do it again if I have to, can't I now?"

She wasn't as sure as she let on to her mam. Two questions kept Meggy tossing and turning and searching for answers all that night. How would she keep Dan safe so far away from home? How could she keep the soldiers from discovering their school again? By morning, Meggy had a plan. She made sure she was first up. As she talked the birdies into giving her their warm eggs, she slipped the master's book into the sack that already contained Dan's slate and her copy-board, which might, at some point serve a finer purpose than practicing spelling. She didn't need any more lessons from Fancy Feet O'Flaherty for what she was planning to do. She added a chunk of cheese and some buttered bread, because now their hedge school was too far away for them to come home for dinner.

Before Da left for the mines, he reminded them of the directions. "Go down the gap, through the oak woods to the twin Monkey Puzzle trees, then follow your nose to the lake and the stony books. Walk smartly, and no lollygaggin' along the way." Mam gave them three more hugs than was her habit. She started to say her usual good-bye, but her voice seemed to get lost in her throat.

Meggy and Dan headed off down the gap, well

before the heavy morning mist lifted. Ragged windows in the mist, revealing peeks of the Purple Mountains, gave them a point to hike toward. Meggy kept turning to look back home, and Mam stood at the door waving with a smile on her face and worry in her eyes, until they disappeared into the woods. Dan, who usually tore off ahead of her or trailed way behind, stayed right by her side and even let her hold his hand. A sudden crackle from the bramble froze them to their spots.

Meggy clutched Dan to her, her eyes desperately searching the woods on either side of the path for soldiers. She couldn't decide which way to run until she located the source of the sound. Dan was so still he might have been a statue. Off to the right, a tall fern rustled and lurched toward them. Meggy took one step to the left, but then she heard Dan give a nervous giggle. There, poking its black face through the feathery ferns, was a spring lamb.

"Look out, Meggy! Officer Lamb is goin' to get you. You were afraid of a wee lamb," teased Danny.

"And I wonder, who was that brave lad holdin' me hand so tight, he left five fine fingernail marks right here?" retorted Meggy as she held out her hand in evidence.

A shared, sheepish sigh of relief ended their teasing and they proceeded down the path with Officer Lamb

bringing up the rear. The woods seemed to go on forever with imagined soldiers or informers ready to leap out at them from behind every towering oak.

Normally, Meggy and Danny lingered in the woods, exploring its treasures. Today, the wild roses that Meggy usually picked for the master bloomed unnoticed. The robin's cheery song went unheard. The goose that Dan normally chased went undisturbed. The sweet perfume of the honeysuckle went unsniffed. The tang of the lake was the only smell they were interested in.

Just when the forest seemed like it would never give way, yellow mustard flowers brightened the edge of the path. Far ahead, down a little hollow, Meggy could see two man-sized silhouettes, shrouded in mist, guarding the path. Were they what she hoped for, or were they what she feared? "Danny, squat here behind this holly patch while I scout out this next bit of path," she ordered in her best big sister voice. Dan grumbled but did as she said.

Being sure to stay on the spongy moss at the side, Meggy tiptoed softly forward a few steps down the path. She squinted her eyes to get a better look at the shadowy guardians ahead. They stood stock still, as if rooted to the earth. She hoped they were. A cool breeze, with a hint of the lake, tore a hole in the mist. These guards had too many protruding limbs to be real

soldiers. They were armed only with their needles. Turning back, Meggy called, "Come Dan, they're the twin Monkey Puzzle trees that Da told us to look for. We're gettin' closer."

The trees seemed like a gateway to safety, for the minute they passed through them, the mist disappeared to reveal a meadow filled with buttercups. Meggy blinked at their sunshiny glory after the gloom of the woods. Dan dashed right into them, the tall buttercups tickling his chin, while Meggy ran to catch up. She was just beginning to fret that he might get lost in this sea of yellow when she caught sight of the Crankanny tree. It stood at the edge of the gently sloping meadow with its gnarly branches beckoning them closer like Gran's crooked fingers. "Race ye to the Crankanny, Dan." They ran so fast, the buttercups were just a yellow blur as they passed. Meggy made sure that they ended in a tie, both hugging the big tree at the same time. Even with both their sets of arms, they couldn't begin to reach all the way round it.

Danny looked up in awe. "Meggy! It is ten times taller than you."

"Danny! It is fifteen times taller than you."

"Meggy, it is eight times taller than your darlin' Robin Hood!"

"Danny, it is even way, way taller than your big old giant, Finn MacCoul!"

"Hall-ooo up there," a familiar voice startled them from their bantering. Meggy and Dan ran to the far side of the tree and looked down. There was the master, standing tall and proud on a huge stack of stony books. As Meggy and Dan slid and skidded down the cliff toward him, the master opened up his arms and called, "Welcome, welcome to our hidin' school."

"Master, Master, ye truly are safe! The soldiers really didn't hurt ye?" asked Meggy, looking up at the master with tear-bright eyes.

"They didn't hurt me. Not at all, at all, sweet Meggy," answered the master as he sat down and gave her a hand up to sit beside him.

"Me too, me too," begged Danny from the bottom. They each took a firm grip of one of his chubby little hands and hauled him up to join them. Breathless for the moment, either from the effort or the beauty of the place, the three sat in shared silence. The magical Lough Leane, backed by the Purple Mountains, sparkled behind them, while the island of Innisfallen seemed to float to the west.

Dan had never been there before, so his urge to explore the stony books soon disturbed the quiet. "Who put them here? What are they made of? How old are they?" he asked in rapid succession, as he clambered up and down the biggest books he'd ever seen.

The master explained, "The black bookcover-like layers are made out of a hard rock called chert. The gray pockmarked page-like layers are limestone, which is made of fish skeletons and seashells from long ago." Danny found the rocky books much more interesting to climb upon than learn about. Meggy, who had visited here with Mam and Da before, loved the stony books. She liked to close her eyes and picture a wise and gentle giantess, like Finn MacCoul's wife, Oonagh, sitting on the top at dusk, reading to all the deer, sheep,

and hedgehogs nestled below her.

At that thought, Meggy's green eyes widened and she looked at the master. "Sir, when the bullies came upon us ye dropped your fine book. I've brought it back to ye, here in my bag. Wouldn't this be a lovely place for ye to sit and read to us of Robin Hood?"

"So it would, Meggy, so it would," answered the master. "You've done such a fine job of carin' for it, that I wonder if you'd mind continuin' to keep it until things settle down again," he added as he jumped down to meet the other students who had appeared on the clifftop.

"Please wait, Sir. I have something to ask you. Will the dance master be visiting us here?" asked Meggy.

"That I do not know, Meggy. Fancy Feet O'Flaherty seems to have vanished," answered Master Cleary. "He was last seen on the road east of town." Seeing the disappointed look on his pupil's face he added, "I know you'll be missin' the dancin', Meggy. Perhaps O'Flaherty will pop up here as mysteriously as he disappeared. Until then, you could show the little ones how to do the beginning steps, couldn't you now?" Meggy nodded with pleasure. "Now run ahead, Dance Mistress MacGillycuddy, and announce your role to the others."

As Master Cleary gathered the class together under the Crankanny tree, Meggy and Fiona hugged and whispered together.

"And who will be our lookout for today?" asked the master seriously. Roddy McSorley had the good grace to keep his hand and his head down, seemingly studying an invisible spot on his boots. As much as Meggy yearned to be the lookout, and even had a special plan, she wouldn't leave Dan's side today, not for a minute. No hands went up. Meggy watched the master as one by one, he searched the faces of the bigger students.

"I'll be the lookout today, Master," volunteered Fiona, as she rose shyly.

"That's a brave lass. And what will your signal be?"

"Well, Meggy has been tellin' me about Officer Lamb who joined them on their journey this mornin', so I think I'll just be a-baaing and a-maaing if necessary."

Danny had a fine time telling the others of the soldier-sheep, the last sight of which had been his little black tail saluting as it disappeared into the field of buttercups. But Meggy didn't join in the laughter. She was watching Fiona disappear to her post past the far side of the Crankanny tree and worrying. "I don't want Fiona to be in danger, but I know she will do a much

better job at lookin' out for us than that big eejit, Roddy McSorley, did."

"Good morning, lads and lassies. And why are you here today?" asked the master, just as if they were back in their snug school in the hedge. After a moment's hesitation, Meggy led the others in responding, "Good morning, Master Cleary. We are here today to exercise our brains."

Only one false alarm occurred during Fiona's watch. It was issued by Officer Lamb.

under the crankanny tree

Each day, Meggy and Dan looked back toward home fewer times. Each day, Mam's eyes held a little less worry. Each day, the sun rose earlier and shrank the blankets of mist that had darkened the woods. Instead of being startled by Officer Lamb's sudden appearances, Meggy and Dan welcomed his woolly company. Instead of rushing fearfully down the path, they lingered a little.

"Listen, Meggy. The robin is singin' just for us," whispered Danny.

"And what is it that she's chirpin', Dan?" asked Meggy.

Hopping up on an old stump, Dan crouched down,

tucked his hands into his armpits and began calling, "Cheerily, cheery-me — she's tellin' us it is time to cheer up now."

Happy to see a smile on her little brother's face, Meggy held out her arms and said, "Cheer-up now, is it? Come, you little redheaded robin, I'll teach ye to fly." And she flew him, chirping all the way, up the path as far as she could carry his definitely not light-as-a-feather-body. The minute his feet hit the ground, Dan was racing ahead looking for toadstools. Every time he found one he had to stop and check underneath for one of the little people.

Watching him play, Meggy thought, "Since the landlord's bullies came, I'm not even sure I believe in the fairies anymore. But I definitely know what I'd wish for, if ever I did catch me one." Right now, she wished her brother would hurry up or they'd be late for school. She scooped Dan up from where he was toadstool-tipping on his hands and knees, and swung him, round and round on the path landing him in the right direction. "Last one to the Monkey Puzzle trees is a monkey's uncle!"

Fairies or not, a special kind of magic happened in the hiding school under the Crankanny tree. Master Cleary's lessons by the lake were the finest he'd ever given, and he'd given many fine ones before. Ireland's history came alive as his passionate voice charged through the clear lake air and ignited the sparks of loyalty and love of country in the hearts and minds of his students.

Botany lessons became treasure hunts as he sent them off searching for hazel, holly, and honeysuckle to identify and draw. Mathematics became a game as the students happily competed in counting off pebbles, waves, and the gulls screeching above. Lookouts, prepared to moo like a cow or caw like a crow for danger, took turns spending quiet days patrolling the cliff and the field.

Meggy relaxed and reveled in each day's chapter of the adventures of Robin Hood. She wasn't the only one. Every child there cheered as Robin stole from the bad and gave to the good. They giggled and squirmed when Robin met his lady-love, Maid Marian, by the trysting tree. When Master Cleary read in a deep romantic voice that Marian "would trade castles and earldoms for Robin's love," Fiona got so caught up in the story that she sighed and said, "Oh, for such a true love." A nearby snicker made her realize she'd spoken aloud and she blushed and hid her face in Meggy's shoulder.

The stories didn't end at story time. It wasn't hard to imagine their woods as the forest hiding place of Little John, Will Scarlet, and the rest of the outlaw band. The older boys ate their dinner on the run as they played out

Robin's adventures. The team who chose the short stick had to be the Sheriff of Nottingham's villainous soldiers. The others became the high-spirited Merry Men, gathering round the Crankanny, which they had declared to be their greenwood tree.

Meggy was the only girl who dared to join them. "If Maid Marian can venture into Sherwood Forest, then so can I." The boys reluctantly allowed her to play and then completely ignored her. All except for Roddy, whether he was one of Robin's band or one of the Sheriff's soldiers, he spent all of his time chasing her. Meggy vowed, "I'd rather kiss one of St. Patrick's snakes than be captured by him."

So she joined Fiona, who was weaving fairy crowns for the little ones from the tall ox-eye daisies growing nearby. Fiona hid her smile and listened patiently as Meggy complained about Roddy. "And wouldn't this place be heaven on earth, if it wasn't for the presence of that big waste of good Irish skin and bones?"

Master Cleary chuckled to himself as he overheard their conversation. He took off his black coat and rolled up the sleeves of his white shirt. Leaning back against the Crankanny, he smiled as he observed all the children of his school playing so happily on the clifftop and below.

Danny's troop of wee giants, armed with driftwood

swords, were marching and chanting, "Hup, two, three, four," as they prepared to conquer the Stony Book Castle.

Meggy called out to the master, "Now aren't those the smallest giants you ever did see?"

"Well now, Meggy, that all depends on the way you're thinkin' about it. In the land of the Lilliputians those wee lads would be giants, wouldn't they now? Perhaps I should be tellin' Gulliver's traveling tales soon."

He looked rather like a giant himself as he stepped carefully through the fairy-crowned crowd. Leaning over Meggy and Fiona he said, "You've done a lovely job of entertainin' the little ones. You'd enjoy a break of your own now, wouldn't you?" Offering each of them a hand, he helped them to their feet. By the time he had the little ones organized in a game of Ring Around the Rosie, the two friends had reached their favorite spot by the water. Hearing some squeals of laughter they looked up to see that Officer Lamb had bunted and baaed his way into the circle.

"Help me practice me sidestep, will ye?" asked Fiona as they climbed up onto the broad, flat rock. Its large, smooth surface gave the girls a fine dance floor; even better than the MacGillycuddy's cottage door when Meggy's da unhinged it and laid it down for them.

Standing straight and tall by Fiona, Meggy said, "Put your heels together, start with your right foot, hop — two, three, four, five, six." Although shy, Fiona was a natural dancer, too. She just lacked Meggy's spirited confidence. "You got it perfect first time. You don't need any more practicin'. Let's dance!"

The dashing of the waves against the rocks gave them the only music that they needed. Soon four legs were leaping in perfect unison. Their raggedy skirts whirled so fast that their shabbiness disappeared in a swish of color. Fiona's fair hair flew straight out from her head like the sail of a boat. Meggy's wild black curls,

bouncing on her shoulders, looked like they were doing a jig of their own.

Meggy and Fiona were so caught up in the shared joy of their dancing, that they didn't notice the audience gathering below until they heard the clapping, led by Roddy. "Is it dancin' that you're wantin'? Well, it's dancin' that you'll get!" called Meggy to her schoolmates. The two girls clasped hands and danced the finest jig ever danced by the shores of Lough Leane. When the others clapped and chanted, "Faster, faster!" they rose to the challenge without missing a beat. Their shoes tapped and turned so quickly that it was impossible to tell whether there were two feet or four. Right in time with the resounding crash of a big wave, they suddenly stopped, bowed, and curtseyed to their cheering fans.

"Thank you, Meggy and Fiona. Your dance demonstration was surely a fine way to end our dinner break. Now I want to be seein' the rest of you dancin' yourselves over to the stony books for the afternoon's lessons," said the master, as he led the way.

That night, safe and snug in their settle bed, Meggy dreamed she was competing with the fastest dance competitor she had ever faced. They were leaping and reeling on the very same rock she and Fiona had danced on that day. First she could see only his feet, and then his long green-clad legs. Could it possibly be . . . ? The roguish smile on his face revealed him to be none other than — Robin Hood.

6

ONE DARK CLOUD

"Meggy, make sure you put your anoraks in your schoolbag today. There is a dark cloud hangin' over The Purples this mornin'," urged Mam.

"Yes, Mam," said Meggy, as she stuffed the bulky sweaters in. Privately, she thought, "A whole sky of blue and Mam is frettin' about one little cloud. Why it could do no more harm than dear little Officer Lamb."

Despite the bright day, the woods still held snatches of mist, snagged like old lace curtains on the branches of the oaks. But by now, their walk through the woods seemed more magical than menacing. Every day Danny got bolder, roving farther off the path and away from

Meggy. Today he was strutting and stomping off through the woods playing giant. Finally, in the deepest part, he disappeared from Meggy's sight and she had to call him back.

"Daniel Joseph Michael MacGillycuddy," she whisper-hollered through the woods, "you come back to me right now!" Nothing but a saucy starling returned her call. Meggy paced the path ten steps forward and ten steps back from her original spot. Each time, she paced faster and called a little louder, "Dan! Dan! Dan-nnny!"

Da had sternly told them both, "Never leave the path, neither of ye, for ye don't know who the woods is hidin'." But Dan wasn't on the path. Should she go into the woods after him, or should she go home to get help?

Deciding to check up and down the path one more time, Meggy hurried forward a little farther to the spot where the tangled willow branches made a dark tunnel over the path. Usually she and Dan threw stones into the darkness to flush out any who might be lurking there. But today she rushed right in. No sooner had she entered than she heard a blood-curdling battle cry, "Aaarrr-gh!" and was knocked to the ground by someone landing on her from above.

Meggy lay stunned and terrified, face-down on the ground. The weight on her back had knocked the wind and the courage right out of her. Suddenly the weight lifted, and a voice said, "Get up, wench. I'm the giant Finn MacCoul, and I've captured you to be me slave."

Before one could say, "Bless us and save us!" Meggy was on her feet. She towered over her brother, looking at him with such anger that he shrank instantly from a giant to a little boy. Gulping for air and trembling with rage, Meggy continued to stare down at him. Dan's shocked eyes locked with hers as he realized his sister had not enjoyed his surprise attack.

When she finally spoke, she didn't sound like Meggy

at all. There was no fun in her voice, only hurt and anger. "Danny, do you not remember what happened not more than a fortnight ago? Do you not remember the soldiers destroyin' our school? Do you not remember you and I runnin' for our lives? Do you not know that those soldiers are still huntin' for us and our master?" Meggy's voice broke only long enough to catch a breath.

"You could have been captured by one of those soldiers today. It is my job to keep you safe. If you choose to leave my sight, even one more time, we will go right home and neither you nor I will ever have lessons by the lake again!"

While Meggy picked up and repacked their school-bag, Dan stood stock still on the path with a single tear running down his cheek. For the first time, Meggy left it unwiped. She simply nodded in the direction of the lake and he walked on, making sure to stay only a step or two ahead of her. By the end of their silent trudge through the woods, they could hear the laughter of their friends floating over the field. Danny took a quick look back at Meggy, but her stern face told him there would be no running through the buttercups today.

This morning, instead of being first as usual, they were last. The others were gathered around the master under the Crankanny tree. "And who will be our lookout for today?"

Meggy's arm shot straight up. "Master, I would be proud to be the lookout." She knew that after what had happened on the path, Dan would be as good as gold, at least for today, in Fiona's capable hands.

"And what will be your signal, Meggy?" asked the master.

Meggy hauled her copy-board out of the bag, placed it on the ground, and in a flurry of intricate foot movements, tapped out a beat. "I'll be dancin' for danger, Master Cleary."

Some of the others more used to kooing and baaing, hooted down Meggy's suggestion. "Dancin' for danger! Have you gone daft, Meggy?"

The master placed his hands on Meggy's shoulders and asked the group, "And who was it that took the cake at the Cake Dance on Saturday night?"

Danny burst out proudly, "It was my sister, Meggy. She's a fine dancer and even a finer sister, because she shared the cake with me!" Everyone laughed at Dan, and even Meggy had trouble hiding a small smile.

The master, taking off his hat and bowing, said, "Introducin', Meggy MacGillycuddy, County Kerry's first and finest dancin' lookout." Meggy made a pretty curtsey and ran off blushing to her lookout point on the field-side of the Crankanny. The rest ran down the cliff

path to begin their day of lessons.

Meggy knew she wouldn't miss any of Robin Hood's adventures today, as she had the book in her apron pocket. She thought, "I'll use the book as my timer. At the end of each page I'll look to each direction, at the end of each chapter I'll walk round the field." As long as there were no soldiers or informers, the looking would be a pleasure with the lake to her face and the buttercup field to her back.

As she read and watched, Meggy could hear snatches of the lessons from below, the older scholars spouting their multiplication tables, and the little ones chanting out their spelling list. Master Cleary's eloquent voice carried his history session up to Meggy. "Look to the island, lads and lassies. There, did no one less than the brave Brian Boru take his schoolin' and learn to be king. You are lucky to be takin' your lessons by the very same lovely lake as he did, aren't you now?"

Meggy smiled as she thought about how the master made history as magical as his stories. He even had them sitting on the west side of the stony books so they could see the island. But as much as she liked her lessons, she was glad to have a bit of quiet time. She rarely had a minute to herself in their small, chore-filled cottage, or during the day when she was responsible for Dan. The lookout job offered her a few rare hours of peace and quiet to read and think.

By the time the sun was near to being straight over-head, she had read four chapters and walked the field four times. Her watchful eyes had not seen even a hint of trouble. She stood up and stretched, ready for a last walk around the field before dinner. Looking down she saw Master Cleary perched on the highest stack, while the children were settled on the stony books around him.

As hard as she tried, Meggy could not hear a sound. She knew the master must be spinning them a frightful yarn. He always spoke in an eerie whisper that sent chills up her spine when he got to a scary part. For a brief moment Meggy wished she were down there, caught up in his storyteller's spell. But she quickly remembered her duty and began to march briskly in the direction of the path.

Just as she was going to round the corner of the field, a dark spot at the far edge of the lake caught her eye. As she watched, it got closer and closer, revealing itself to be a lone man in a boat. Stopping at the cove just to the east of theirs, he got out a telescope and began peering in the direction of the stony books. Meggy flew back to the edge of the cliff by the Crankanny. She threw her copy-board on the ground and danced out her warning. The master stopped his story immediately and turned her way. All eyes looked straight up at her. She pointed to the east and the intruder. The master following the direction of her arm, took one quick look and calmly, but firmly, told the others, "Off with you! Keep crouched down as you climb the cliff and hide behind the Crankanny."

Meggy helped haul the frightened little ones over the top and sent them to huddle in the shade of the tree. But even before the bigger ones climbed all the way up, the boat started to move slowly off in the direction it had come. "Ah Meggy, you had us climbing for nothin' but a wee man in a wee boat," complained one cranky climber.

"Meggy, could it be that you gave out your false alarm because you were longin' for some fine male company?" asked Roddy McSorley with a smug grin on his face. Meggy's blush of anger was seen by the others as the blush of a crush, and they had a good laugh at her expense.

The master took the attention away from her by declaring, "Tis always wiser to be safe than sorry. Now let's take an early dinner break." This sent them all charging back down the cliff path to get their school-bags, left at the bottom in their panic.

By the time they returned for their meal under the Crankanny, Meggy had taken up her lookout post at the far end of the field where she had first spotted the intruder. She kept her back firmly turned away from the others and fumed, "They can all laugh at me, but I will continue to take my job seriously, no matter what they say."

Fiona and Dan brought over her share of the bread and butter and tried to cheer her up. Fiona said, "Don't let that big-mouthed amadon get to ye, Meggy."

Danny echoed, "Yeah, don't let that big-mouthed amadon get to ye." Then he looked up at them and asked, "What is a big-mouthed amadon?"

Together Meggy and Fiona uttered a sigh of shared female exasperation. Fiona answered Dan with a smile. "It's a lazy lout, you silly goose." After agreeing to meet at the Monkey Puzzle trees at the end of the day, Fiona led Dan back to the group.

Near the end of a peaceful afternoon spent reading and watching, Meggy shrugged into her anorak and was grateful the dark cloud had been the only intruder for the rest of her watch.

7

a second chance

Not one dark cloud marred the clear blue sky. The rays of sunshine reached into the woods and lit the dewdrops like crystals on a chandelier. The crab apple trees, top-heavy with pink blossoms, bowed down along the path like ladies-in-waiting, honoring their passing. And Meggy could enjoy every beautiful moment of it because Dan was staying as close to her as a shadow.

As the sweet scent of the wild roses wafted by, Meggy and Dan said at exactly the same time, "Let's pick a bouquet for Mam." They laughed and decided to wait until their trip home so the blooms would be at their

finest. Meggy pointed at a tall plant with bell-shaped flowers and said, "Look Dan, there are the Fairy Fingers. We'll pick some of them later, too, so I can make up more of their Itch Away." The last batch had so soothed Dan's thorn scratches that they soon disappeared.

When they reached the yellow field, Dan tentatively held out his hand to his sister. She rewarded his fine behavior by clasping his little hand in hers. "Come Dan, let's dance with the buttercups." Meggy led him on a rollicking romp through the flowers. He could barely keep up as she skipped him through the field. When she spun and twirled him under her arm he called, "More, Meggy, more!" Meggy grabbed his other hand and they reeled round and round with their heads thrown back until they were so dizzy, they fell down on their backs, panting and giggling.

Dan pointed and said, "Look, Meggy, the buttercups and the sun have made us our own perfect, bright little world." Meggy smiled over at him and they lay quietly, basking in the golden light.

From a distance, Master Cleary's voice reminded them of their destination. Jumping up, they burst through the meadow in front of the others playing round the Crankanny. The fine weather had them all full of high spirits and the master had to call, "Lads and lassies!" three times, until he finally got their attention. "Now, important matters first. Who will be volunteerin' to be our lookout for today?"

Suddenly, all the bigger students got very busy inspecting their nails, or books, or the day's dinner in their bags. Their eyes looked anywhere except at the master. The lessons by the lake were too much fun, and the weather too fine, to be spending the day all alone pacing the field above. "Well, this is a fine day for the lads and lassies of County Kerry. Not a one of you brave enough to watch out for the rest of us, is there now?"

challenged the master.

Meggy wasn't feeling particularly brave, but still smarting a bit from yesterday's teasing about her so-called false alarm, she wanted a second chance. "It's me that'll be takin' the lookout position again today, Master Cleary." She announced this so fiercely that no one dared comment, except for the cheeky Roddy, who gave a sly wink behind her back.

As everyone else headed down the hill, Meggy felt a bit left out. She could hear them chasing the waves and each other until Master Cleary settled them into their lessons. "Well, Meggy MacGillycuddy, you volunteered yourself for a day alone, and now you might as well be makin' the best of it," she scolded herself as she returned to her reading, watching, and walking routine.

Soon the adventures of Robin Hood, especially those he had with Maid Marion, made her forget the adventures she might be missing below. When a chapter ended with Marion donning boys' clothing to join Robin in an archery contest right under the sheriff's nose, Meggy was sorely tempted to skip her lookout duties, just once, to find out what happened. But she reminded herself that Robin and Marion's enemies existed only in the pages of the book, while their own enemies were only too real.

It was a good thing, too, because by the time she got

to the very corner where she had spotted yesterday's lone boatman, she could see not one, but two boats in that same cove. Meggy spent only a split second wondering if this could be another false alarm, for these boats were not stopping. They were heading straight in their direction.

Racing to the far side of the Crankanny, Meggy flung down her copy-board and stomped her feet louder than she'd ever stomped before. She wanted to yell too, because now she could see that the rapidly approaching boats were being rowed by the landlord's troop. But if she yelled, her voice would carry out over the lake and give away their exact location. The children below were being so rowdy that they did not hear her stomping. She tried to send her warning to Master Cleary, who was the only one facing her way, by staring at him with all her might. Finally, he looked up and followed her pointing arm to the approaching danger. He told the others, "Meggy has issued a warning!"

A rude voice interrupted, "Not another of Meggy's false alarms!"

Ignoring the comment, the master went on quickly, "Yesterday's man must have been an informer. There are now two boatloads of soldiers approachin'. Hurry! Climb the cliff path and race through the woods for home. Stop for nothin' and wait for no one. Godspeed."

One look at the quickly approaching boats silenced the children and they rushed, white-faced to the narrow path. Meggy went straight to the cliff edge to help haul them up. Her eyes raced up and down the crush of climbing children, looking for Danny. There he was, just ahead of Fiona, his little hands clawing up the cliff side and his sturdy legs scrambling at such a speed that only the child ahead of him held him back.

As soon as she got Dan safely over the edge, Fiona joined Meggy in pulling the other little ones up. Each small face that appeared at the top was dirt-covered and fear-filled. Then Roddy's big face appeared. Before Meggy could sputter her outrage at him saving himself ahead of some of the smaller children, he said, "The master sent me up to guard and guide the little ones through the woods, but I'll stay and help ye haul a few of the bigger ones up first." Though she would never have admitted it, Meggy was grateful for his help.

With only the master still to come, Roddy led the little ones off through the field toward the path. Meggy and Fiona, holding on to Dan between them, were just ready to make a run for it when Meggy took a look back. She saw the master pushing and rolling a huge rock to the top of the path before giving it a final shove. Meggy cheered silently as she heard soldier after soldier shouting and cursing as it bowled them over. She

thought, "Hooray for Master Cleary, that will give us a good start!"

The master rose and turned back toward her. He had not taken even a step when a shot rang out. Just as he saw Meggy, a look of shock came over his face, and he fell like a log to the ground. Meggy's mouth formed a scream, but not a sound left her lips as she shoved Fiona and Danny into the field and then ran to her master's side. A terrible blossom of red bloodied the arm of his white shirt.

8

Dancing for Danger

"Master, Master wake up!" His lids fluttered open to reveal pained blue eyes in his chalk-white face. Meggy could hear the soldiers finding their way around the boulder that blocked the path to the top of the cliff. A quick glance behind her revealed that the buttercups had swallowed up any trace of Danny and Fiona.

"Master, get up! You must get up!" In a daze, the master followed her commands. He let her pull him up, and staggered to his feet. "You are not strong enough to reach the woods. We must hide in the meadow for now," whispered Meggy, as she flung his good arm over her shoulder and half-carried him to the yellow field.

Now, the buttercups may have been up to Dan's chin, but the master was a tall man and the flowers went only to his waist. Meggy ducked down and dragged him with her. He uttered a muffled moan as his wounded arm hit the ground. Meggy flinched too, as she shared his pain. "Can you crawl, Master?" He nodded mutely. "Follow me then, away from the woodspath to the far edge of the field. They won't be expectin' us there."

Meggy uttered a silent prayer that the soldiers wouldn't notice the buttercups parting as she and the master crawled between them. Little did she know that Master Cleary, moving painfully behind her on two knees and one hand, was uttering the same prayer. Just then, a gust from the lake blew up and set every buttercup in the field bobbing. It was a good thing, too, because the master suddenly groaned and collapsed in an unconscious heap.

Meggy stifled a gasp as she saw that the bloody bloom on his upper arm had turned into a river of red all the way down his sleeve. She turned him over and lifted his head up onto her lap. Then she worked her fingers furiously to release the green ribbon Mam had tied in her hair what seemed like a lifetime ago, but had only been that morning. The master didn't even gain consciousness when she knotted her ribbon as tight as she could above his wound. "At least he has been saved that pain," she thought.

Meggy could hear the soldiers puffing and planning as they gathered at the top of the cliff. She breathed a sigh of relief as she heard one shout, "Look over by those two strange trees. There's a path. We'll catch that law-breaking teacher and those Irish urchins yet."

But her relief for the master and herself was short-lived as she thought of Danny and Fiona, "Please, please, don't let them be waitin' for me. Please, let them be well on their way home."

The master stirred and Meggy knew she must take advantage of the soldiers' time in the woods to get him to a safer spot. "Master Cleary, we must make a dash for the bushes at the corner of the meadow." Somehow, Meggy got him there and propped him up against a small birch surrounded by a thicket, before he blacked out again.

Meggy's mind dashed off in a dozen different directions as she tried to come up with a plan. "How can I get help for Master Cleary without leavin' him alone and unprotected? Even if I could leave him, how would I get down the path to home without bein' captured meself?" As the sun streaked sideways from the west through the bushes, she realized the afternoon was wearing on and there was a chill in the air. She busied herself by making a blanket of dry leaves to cover the master right up to his chin.

She didn't notice him struggling to open his eyes until he spoke. His first words were for her sake. "Meggy, there are no soldiers about now. You must escape."

"No, Master, I'll not be leavin' ye," she said softly but firmly.

"Meggy, I am still your master and you must do as I say — not just for your sake, but for mine, too. I'll need strong helpers to aid me in escapin' from here. I'll need food, water, and a blanket, as I'll have to stay in hidin' till the danger dies down. You are my only hope of gettin' what I need to survive. You'll go for me, won't you, Meggy?"

Meggy couldn't say no to her master any longer. She nodded her reluctant acceptance. They began to make plans. As she tucked her anorak over his shoulders she insisted, "At least you must take this, and our bread and butter."

The master sighed, "Thank you, Meggy. All I have to offer is my advice. Stay off the path, but close to it. Remember, the landlord's bullies may be bigger than you, but you have a bright mind and a brave Irish heart."

A loud voice interrupted their whispered planning. "Aaagh! Even the trees in this heathen country are evil." At the edge of the path stood one angry soldier, rubbing his scowling face where he'd had a run-in with the prickly Monkey Puzzle trees. When he looked up, he seemed to stare straight across the field to where Meggy and Master Cleary were hidden. He started stomping toward them, looking even fiercer than the evil Sheriff of Nottingham.

"Meggy, you must run — now," pleaded the master in a weak voice. Meggy knew if she didn't go, they would both be caught. But how could she leave her beloved master? He looked up at her and said, "Please,

Meggy. The best you can do for me now is to save yourself and dance at me wake."

At the word "dance", Meggy's eyes lit up with hope
and she whispered mysteriously, "Don't worry, Master.
This one doesn't have a gun — I'll take the cake for ye."
And bending over like a black-haired bullet, she blasted
through the buttercups. Popping up in the middle of
the field, facing the surprised soldier, Meggy clapped,
danced a little jig, and then disappeared.

The soldier stood stunned, not sure of what he'd

seen. Then, he changed direction and tromped over the buttercups to where the jigging apparition had appeared. No sooner did he reach the middle, than there she was again. This time she was in the far corner, not only a-spinning and a-whirling, but singing too.

I never did intend a soldier's lady for to be
I never will marry a soldier-O.

"Stop! By the power of the Penal Code, I order you to stop!" he shouted.

Meggy stopped just long enough to duck down and become nothing more than the breeze tossing the yellow blooms.

When Master Cleary heard Meggy's sweet voice singing out, he wondered if his wound was causing him to hear things that could not be. "That canna be Meggy," he thought. "She should be well away by now."

The soldier had only taken a few clumsy steps toward the far corner, when the black-haired beastie spun up dancing and singing away behind him.

I never did intend to go to a foreign land.
I never will leave my Mammy-O.

He was beginning to wonder if the pub tales he'd heard about this country's fairies, who could take whatever size or shape they wanted, were true. As he turned around to grab her, the tall plants snarled around his heavy boots and he fell face-first in the field.

Meggy thought, "Now's my chance." She burrowed straight through the buttercups to the Crankanny. A quick glance revealed the soldier to be down on his hands and knees struggling to untangle himself from the knotty flowers. She scooted up the massive trunk. The dear old tree seemed to lift her up, up, and up into its gnarly branches. Its clumps of long leaves drew a green curtain between her and her enemy's eyes.

The silence was as painful to the master as his gunshot wound. His ears ached for the sound of Meggy's voice. Where was she? Had the soldier captured her? He now realized that the dear, brave girl was risking her life to save his.

The soldier, having finally disentangled himself, was now standing in the middle of the field turning round and round like a weather rooster in a windstorm. "I know you're here, you wild Irish banshee. You'll not get away from me."

Master Cleary breathed a sigh of relief. At least Meggy was still free.

Meggy's lofty nest offered her a safe lookout where she could see if the evil enemy came close to discovering her dear master. She thought, "I must make a plan. I'll break off some chunks of this flaky bark. If that horrible man goes anywhere near my poor, hurt master, I'll throw them out in different directions and draw his attention back this way."

But not even considering that a young girl might have outsmarted him, the soldier continued to search and re-search only the part of the field where he had last seen her.

9

in the dark of the woods

At dusk, the frustrated soldier stood directly below the Crankanny muttering, "A curse on that wild Irish girl and this heathen country that hides her from me."

High above him, Meggy was repeating over and over in her head, "Stay calm, be still; stay calm, be still." She was petrified that if she moved so much as a cramped muscle, the gnarly old branch she was perched upon would creak and reveal her hiding place.

Poor, wounded Master Cleary had slipped again into unconsciousness and was unaware of the terrible danger Meggy was in.

A deafening crash of thunder suddenly rolled in off

the lake. The soldier jumped as if a giant had roared right into his ear. And although Meggy was used to County Kerry's almost daily rainstorms, the sudden almighty noise, combined with the stress of the day, shocked her into losing her foothold.

Feeling herself falling, Meggy clawed desperately at the flaky bark of the branch. Pieces of it broke off in her hands and joined the rain pelting down on the soldier's head. Uneasily he looked up, just as a flash of lightning revealed the wild hair, white face, and flailing legs of the dancing apparition, ready to pounce on him from above. He was so spooked, he took off screaming in panic — "Aye-yie-yie!" — as he stumbled down the steep cliff with nothing but his own fear chasing him.

The same flash of lightning showed Meggy his cowardly face. Seeing his terror, she let out a few shrieks and called after him in a banshee-like voice, "Come dance with me. Come dance with me. I'll dance ye to your grave!" This made the lout run all the faster, until all that Meggy could see of him was his bouncing backside disappearing into the gloom.

Meggy realized this was her chance to move. But how? Looking down, she quickly considered her options. "If I jump from this high up, there'll be nothing but Meggy mush left of me at the bottom. I'll have to make my way, hand over hand, along the branch to

the trunk. But saints above, I don't know if I have the strength to do it."

When she tried, her right hand seemed to be paralyzed. Desperately, Meggy willed it to move. Not so much as a baby finger twitched. With all her concentration focused on her right hand, it finally made its move to cross over the left. As all her weight pulled on her already aching shoulder, Meggy gritted her teeth. Bit by bit, she inched her way along the branch. Reaching the heart of the Crankanny, she hugged it with all her might. As she shimmied down its wide trunk, the tree offered her footholds like stair steps to guide her way.

Meggy's legs were so wobbly when she hit the ground that she had to hold onto the tree until she stopped shaking. Before she left the security of the Crankanny, she looked about. There was neither sight nor sound of the soldier. For a split second Meggy debated, "Should I go check on the master, or should I head straight out for help?" As much as she hated her own answer, she knew she could do more for Master Cleary by leaving him. The thought of him hurt and now wet, sent her hurrying through the field.

Through the gray dusk she could just make out the strange silhouettes of the Monkey Puzzle trees. By the time she reached them and the path, it was dark. Meggy

had never been in the woods at night. As she started
off down the path, she remembered the master's words.
"Stay off the path, but keep close to it."

But those words conflicted with Da's stern rule.
"Never leave the path, neither of ye, for ye don't know
who the woods are hidin'."

Meggy thought, "I think me feet know their way
down the path, even in this dark. But if I go into the
woods I may get lost." As she stood there trying to
decide, a bolt of lightning lit up the forest. It was like a

dozen lanterns were suddenly turned right on her. Her white apron seemed to glow in the dark.

Meggy jumped off the path and hid behind a crab apple tree. The smell of its sweet blossoms comforted her as she tore off her apron, lifted her skirts, and tied it on again underneath, making sure the precious book was safe in her pocket.

The scent of the crab apples gave Meggy an idea. "I know the smells of the trees and plants along the path, and this rain is drippin' them into the air like a fine lady's perfume. If I stay just off the edge of the path, I can sniff my way home." Focusing on the smells also helped take Meggy's mind off her fear of being alone in the nightwoods. Her nose led her a good distance, past wild garlic and the honeysuckle.

Once she was off the footpath and hidden by the trees and bushes, the lightning became her friend instead of her enemy. Its occasional flashes briefly lit the way and helped her not to stray too far into the woods.

Suddenly, she was surrounded by a deep, damp darkness. Chills went up Meggy's spine as wet tentacles slapped her face and slithered round her head. Trying not to scream, her breath escaped her mouth in little gasps as she reached up to rip the slimy offenders away. But when she dared to tear the first one off her face, she realized what it was. "I'm in the willow tunnel. It is scary enough in the daytime. Tonight it feels like a giant sea monster hangin' over me."

Bursting out of the tunnel, she was greeted by what looked like huge, white eyeballs with staring yellow pupils, suspended about two feet above the ground. Meggy's nature-loving eyes, trained by Master Cleary's botany lessons, recognized the ox-eye daisies lining the path. "Thank goodness these daisies, unlike their lazy English cousins, bloom all night," Meggy whispered. When she stepped back into the woods again, she could still follow the petalled lanterns a good way further. The scent of the Fairy Fingers told her she was more than halfway home.

A sudden snuffly sound stopped Meggy in her tracks. Was that a soldier's sneeze? She tried to locate the sound, which seemed to be coming from near her feet. As the snuffling came closer, Meggy thought, "Tis highly unlikely that a soldier with a cold is crawlin' on his belly on the ground."

A flash of lightning revealed a roly-poly hedgehog sniffing out his nightly meal of slugs and snails. The thought of a meal, combined with a gentle whiff of wild roses, made Meggy think of Mam and home. Her eyes blurred with tears and she wiped them away quickly with the hem of her skirt. Looking up, she saw what seemed to be the light of a lantern, swinging way too

high to be any daisy. Hearing male voices, she ducked down behind the rose bushes. "Thank goodness I heeded the master's advice and stayed off the path," thought Meggy, as the lantern light broke through the darkness all around her.

Meggy shook her head in disbelief and listened carefully to the voices. There it was again! "Could that voice really be callin' me name? Could it really be me da?" Not until he was standing right on the path in front of her, with the lantern lighting his rugged face, did

Meggy feel safe enough to rise up out of the roses and reveal herself.

"Meggy, love! Where have you been? Your mam has been half mad with worry since Fiona and Dan came home without ye." Taking a good look at her fear-haunted face, Da stopped his scolding and gathered her into his strong miner's arms.

"Da! Da! They shot Master Cleary. I hid him — he needs help." Meggy's words tumbled out as fast as the tears rolled down her cheeks.

"Slow down, love. Fiona told us the master was hurt. Tell us more," urged Da, as Meggy realized that Roddy and his father were standing behind him with their own lantern. "Where is he hid? How bad is he hurt? The brazen brutes are down at our pub braggin' about doin' away with him!"

"They've got nothin' to be braggin' about!" Meggy burst out angrily through her tears. "They shot him when his back was turned. He needs help now! I'll take you to him." She turned and started back down the path.

Her father's long arm reached out and pulled her back. "No, Meggy. This is not a job for you. We're close to home. I'll see you safe there first. We'll have to be hidin' Master Cleary away for a while till he mends, and the soldiers move on. We've brought him bandages, blankets, and food supplies. Just tell Roddy and his father where you hid your master and they'll go ahead to him. I'll catch up to them later."

Meggy's face was filled with hurt and anger, "But Da . . ."

"No buts, Meggy."

10

the banshee's tale

"Excuse me, Sir," interrupted Roddy, "but hasn't Meggy been the bravest of us all and sure, wouldn't we be findin' Master Cleary faster if she was with us?"

"Me lad's got a good point there, MacGillycuddy," said Roddy's father. "Every minute saved could mean life or death to the master."

Meggy could never remember her da changing his mind once he'd made a decision. She held her breath waiting for him to speak. When he finally looked at her, it was with the confused look of a father who had sent his little girl off to school in the morning, and had now discovered a brave young woman standing in her place, almost eye to eye with him.

Meggy's green eyes held all the answers he needed. In them he saw bravery, strength, and most of all, love. He spoke abruptly, giving orders. "I'll lead the way. Meggy, you stay right behind me, so you can be givin' me directions as I need them. Roddy, you guard Meggy's back. McSorley, use your lantern to watch that no one sneaks up on us from the rear."

Meggy was so surprised by Roddy's support and her da's change of mind, that she swallowed her complaints before they spilled out of her mouth. The words, *I should be leadin'*, and *I have definitely proved I don't need Roddy guardin' me back*, felt like they were boring holes in her teeth trying to get out. She clamped her mouth firmly shut and stepped silently into her place — second in line.

With the lantern lighting the way, the trip back down the path was fast and easy compared to her dark journey up it. Her father spoke only once. "Meggy, you needn't worry about the soldiers. Me mates have cooked up a plan to be keepin' them at the pub for the night."

Meggy did worry, though. "Should I warn Da about the lone soldier? If I do, he'll likely be takin' me back home. I'll tell him at the Monkey Puzzles. That should be soon enough."

Roddy was tromping so close behind her that he

stepped on her heel, pulling her shoe off. Out of force
of habit, Meggy turned around to scowl up at him. But
he wasn't towering over her as usual. He was down on
one knee, slipping her shoe back on before she could
even jerk her foot away.

"Sorry, Meggy. Me feet are growin' so fast these days
that I don't seem to have any say-so over where they
go," apologized Roddy, as he looked up at her. He
seemed so truly sorry that she forgot, for a minute, that
she thought him "a big amadon" and remembered how
he'd spoken up to her father on her behalf, and the way

84

he'd helped the little ones today.

She asked him, "Roddy, did you get all the little ones home safe and sound? Did you see Danny and Fiona?"

As he stood up, they resumed walking and he answered her simply, "Meggy, they're all back in their mams' arms now. I saw that your mother had Dan and Fiona all wrapped up snug in blankets and sippin' warm milk by the hearth when we stopped by to pick up your da."

Meggy smiled gratefully up at him for sharing such fine news.

Roddy asked, "Will ye be tellin' me about Master Cleary now, Meggy?"

"It happened right after you left with the little ones. The sound of the shot — the blood — the master falling. Oh, Roddy! It's too awful for words," said Meggy, as she began to shake.

"No more now, Meggy. There's no need to tell me more. We'll get to Master Cleary in time. We'll get him to safety," said Roddy in a comforting voice she'd never heard him use before.

The light of the lanterns changed the whole look of the woods. The glow robbed even Meggy's sea monster of its scary gloom. By the time the Monkey Puzzle trees showed up in the lamplight, the rain had stopped falling. Meggy knew that for everyone's safety she couldn't delay her telling any longer. "Da, don't go any farther."

Her father turned around and said impatiently, "What is it, Meggy?"

Meggy got up her nerve and spat it out, "Da, there is a lone, unarmed soldier somewhere round here. He chased me through the buttercups while I led him away from the master's hidin' place. I last saw him under the Crankanny."

Da's mouth hung open as a flurry of emotions flew across his face — anger, fear, shock.

Before he could decide how to feel or what to say, Mr. McSorley offered a solution. "I'll go on a bit with you and then stand lookout for the brute, while you tend to the master." Da took one long look at sturdy, dependable Mr. McSorley and nodded.

Roddy asked in a low whisper, "Meggy, where did you hide the master?"

Meggy pointed to the corner of the field, in a straight line across from the Monkey Puzzles and said, "I left him there. Pray that he is still there, and still alive."

Crouching low, they moved across the edge of the field as quickly and quietly as possible. When Meggy spotted the birch and the thicket, she could hold back no longer. She ran ahead of her da to where the master lay. Even knowing where she'd left him, it was hard to

see him now. Da's lantern over her shoulder revealed a long, low mound of soaking wet leaves. As Da swung the lantern forward, Meggy could see Master Cleary's still, gray face.

She dropped down on her knees beside him. One of the master's hands appeared as she disturbed the leaves. Meggy took hold of it. It was as cold as clay. Holding back a sob, she began rubbing the limp hand in her own. The big man and the big lad behind her stood speechless, not knowing what to do or say. She started tearing the wet leaves off the master's still body, yelling, "Don't just stand there. Do somethin'! Help me get him warm."

As she turned back to her desperate work, the other two looked at each other hopelessly. First Da, then Roddy dropped to their knees and did what they could. "I'll help ye get these wet leaves away and then cover him with this dry blanket," offered Da.

"I'll take his wet boots off and rub his feet," said Roddy.

After one quick sweep of his lantern in the master's direction, Mr. McSorley turned back to his silent watch and prayed to the saint of lost causes.

"How do I tell me brave girl the words she doesn't want to hear?" wondered Da, as he searched desperately for the right thing to say. He leaned across to clasp

Meggy's hands when she suddenly sat up, perfectly still, staring at the master's face. Following her gaze, Da saw what she saw. The master's bright blue eyes were shining up at them. He was trying to say something. His mouth moved, but no sound came out. He tried again. Meggy leaned right over him so she could hear what might be her beloved master's last words.

When she turned to share these words with the others, she was both crying and laughing so hard, they thought she'd gone mad. Finally she got his words out. "The master asks, 'Roddy, are you tryin' to steal me fine boots?'"

Roddy started to sputter his denial, until he saw the twinkle in Master Cleary's eyes. "Master, you're — you're alive!"

"Aye, Roddy. There is still a spark of life in your teacher yet," said the master in a voice as dry as the crackle of old leaves.

"The man needs a drink, Roddy. Fetch the flask," ordered Da. He lifted the master's head gently up in his big arms to help him take a sip.

After searching through the pack, Meggy gave some instructions of her own. "Mr. McSorley, would you kindly be lowerin' your lantern a little so I can check the master's arm? Roddy, press hard here, while I untie the ribbon and dress the wound with the clean bandages Mam sent. Master, you try to get down some of this broth that Da is goin' to feed ye. It will warm your inners and give you some strength." When Meggy finished up by wiping his face with a damp cloth, Master Cleary looked much more alive than dead.

Da tried to take charge again. "Master Cleary, now that you're feelin' a bit better, the McSorleys will be movin' ye to a hideout where ye may heal in safety, and I'll be takin' Meggy home."

But it was now the master's turn and he spoke in his teacher's voice, which even grown men knew better than to interrupt. "Not quite yet, my good man. There are some things that need sayin'. First, Roddy, how are the little ones?"

"I did just as you asked, Master. They were good as gold as I guided them through the woods. You'd have been proud of them all."

"Aye Roddy, I am proud of them, and of you, too. You have the makin's of a fine man, and I thank ye for your service to your fellow students and meself."

"And wasn't Fiona a fine and obedient girl to run straight home with our Dan?" pointed out Meggy's da.

"Yes, and sure you have a daughter to be very proud of yourself, you know, Mr. MacGillycuddy. Meggy and her dancin' saved me life today," stated Master Cleary, looking at Meggy, his face filled with gratitude.

The others, especially Da, looked at him, and then Meggy with great confusion. But the master continued speaking before they could ask even one question.

"Before we part ways, I must tell you a tale that began today in this field, and will live on by the hearths of County Kerry forever. From this night forward, it will be called *The Dancin' Banshee*. Its heroine will belong to the people of Kerry as one of their own, a lovely lass with raven-black hair and laughin' green eyes. She was known for lovin' three things: her wee brother, her larnin', and her dancin'. But when enemies tried to destroy that which she held dear, she fought back with the power of her love, her mind, and her dancin' feet.

"There will be some, especially those with treacherous hearts, who will never step foot near the stony books again, for they will swear that at dusk they can hear a strange voice screamin' up and down the cliff.

"There will be more, many more, with passion in their hearts and magic in their feet, who will return here on stormy nights, hopin' to catch a glimpse of her in the flashes of lightnin' so that they, too, can join in the wondrous spell of her dancin'.

"There will be one young lad who will grow to an old man, tellin' all who will listen about his sister, who could dance like the wind and was as brave as the giant, Finn MacCoul.

"And meself, I'll never forget the darlin' green-eyed banshee who saved me life and danced her way into me heart forever."

Meggy's eyes shone bright with pride as she added, "And, Master, long after me black curls turn to silver, I will return here when the buttercups are bloomin'. I'll dance in their yellow, and then rest and remember, with me back to the Crankanny and me face to the waves."

acknowledgements

I would like to acknowledge P. J. Dowling's book, *The Hedge Schools of Ireland*, Mercier Press 1968, which has been a valuable source of information throughout the writing of this story.

For an author, sending a book proposal off to a publisher ranks right up there on the anxiety scale with sending your little child off to school for the first time. Sending your fledgling manuscript off to Kathryn Cole is like hoping your child will get the best teacher in the whole school. My hopes have been realized.

After one of our editing sessions Kathryn said to me, "Thanks, that was fun." And it was fun, because this editor came to my words with vision, talent, respect, humor, and heart.

Margot Griffin was an award-winning teacher who is now a journalist and author. She writes a syndicated column called *Ask the Book Lady*, which appears regularly in Canadian newspapers. Margot has traveled to Ireland and visited the locations in this story. Her own Irish roots and love of the people, shine through in Meggy's adventure. A great promoter of family literacy, she lives with her husband and daughter in a storybook cottage in London, Ontario. *Dancing for Danger* is Margot's first book, but it will soon be followed by another exciting Meggy Tale.

P. John Burden is a builder, architectural model maker, stained glass craftsman, and book illustrator. He has worked on a number of books including *A Horse Called Farmer*, *Lena and the Whale*, and *Spike Chiseltooth*. He created the illustrations for this book on his computer. John lives on Prince Edward Island.